Blue Is My Name!

by Angela C. Santomero
illustrated by Karen Craig

Ready-to-Read™

Simon Spotlight/Nick Jr.

New York London Toronto Sydney Singapore

NOTE TO PARENTS

Welcome to the first in a series of Ready-to-Read books done the Blue's Clues way! This line of books has been researched with preschoolers to ensure a high level of interactivity in this simple rebus format. Preschoolers are encouraged to read along with you by reading the pictures above the words in this story. Because the word is also underneath each picture, your preschooler will begin to recognize and learn each word as well! What's more, this line of books is reminiscent of Blue's journal. Each story has been written from Blue's own preschooler point of view and reveals her innermost feelings about the world around her.

To Traci Paige Johnson: Thank you for being a true visionary, a very best friend, and the cutest Blue puppy in the world. I look forward to the next ten years together!—A. C. S.

To my family—K. C.

Based on the TV series *Blue's Clues* ® created by Traci Paige Johnson, Todd Kessler, and Angela C. Santomero as seen on Nick Jr. ®
On *Blue's Clues,* Steve is played by Steven Burns.

SIMON SPOTLIGHT
An imprint of Simon & Schuster Children's Publishing Division
1230 Avenue of the Americas, New York, New York 10020

Copyright © 2000 Viacom International Inc.
All rights reserved. NICKELODEON, NICK JR., *Blue's Clues*, and all related titles, logos, and characters are trademarks of Viacom International Inc.

All rights reserved including the right of reproduction in whole or in part in any form.
READY-TO-READ, SIMON SPOTLIGHT, and colophon are registered trademarks of Simon & Schuster.

Manufactured in the United States of America
8 10 9

Library of Congress Cataloging-in-Publication Data
Santomero, Angela C.
Blue is my name / by Angela C. Santomero ; illustrated by Karen Craig. —
1st ed.
p. cm. — (Ready-to-read)
Based on the TV series Blue's clues created by Traci Paige Johnson, Todd Kessler, and Angela C. Santomero as seen on Nick Jr.
Summary: Blue loves being blue because it is the color of the sky, her favorite bird, water, and other wonderful things. Features rebuses.
ISBN 0-689-83122-6 (pbk.)
1. Rebuses. [1. Blue Fiction. 2. Rebuses.] I. Craig, Karen, ill.
II. Blue's clues (Television program) III. Title. IV. Series.
PZ7.S23825Bl 2000
[E]—dc21
99-16406

Hi, It's me, ! BLUE

I'm so HAPPY to see you.

Blue

BLUE
is my name.
Do you know why?
B
L
U
E

Because  is the color of the  .

BLUE

SKY

BLUE is the color of
my favorite  in
BIRD
a  . The bird's
TREE
 like me, can
BLUE
you see?

is the color of the
BLUE
in my .
WATER
BATHTUB

BLUE is the color
of my TOWEL .

Rub! Rub! Rub!

hat
Steve

Blue is the CRAYON that
I always choose,

when I write the number 222.

TWO

BLUE is also the color of my RAINHAT and SHOES !

is found in my
BLUE
favorite .
PANCAKES

Just like the ones

makes!

MR. SALT

Shake! Shake! Shake!

is my name.
I'm proud, don't
you see...

because is
BLUE
the color of me!